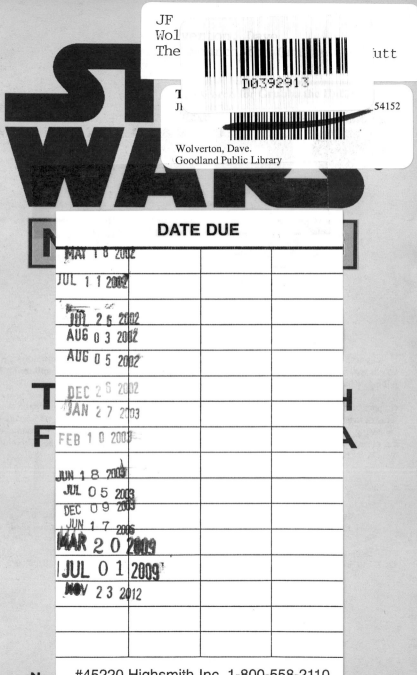

ISBN 0-590-10952-9

12 11 10 9 8 7 6 5 4 3 2   8 9/9 0 1 2/0

Printed in the U.S.A.

First Scholastic printing, February 1998

PRELIMINARY MISSION

CHAPTER ONE

"Look, big nose, I hear you know where Grubba the Hutt has been taken, and you're going to tell me right now, or you'll be scraping your snout off the ceiling!"

Han Solo had the Kubaz spy in his grasp, inside a booth at the Mos Eisley cantina. The Kubaz, a gray-skinned alien with a long trunk, was much stronger than Solo had thought he would be. But the alien quit struggling once he had a blaster shoved into his face.

Solo was shaking with rage, and his partner Chewbacca put a restraining hand on Solo's shoulder. Solo had saved Jabba's Ur-Damo, Grubba the Hutt, from kidnappers only days before. He'd hoped that by returning the young Hutt to Jabba, he'd get some kind of reward — enough so that Jabba would take the bounty off Solo's head. But after he'd landed here on Tatooine, Grubba had been kidnapped again. Solo needed to get Grubba back — fast.

"I cannot tell you where Grubba has been taken," the Kubaz said, twisting his gray head to the side. He wore a deep-hooded robe and goggles, and spoke through an electronic translator that made his voice sound tinny and mechanical. "I cannot betray a hive-mate."

"I'll give you to the count of three, and then I pull the trigger," Solo said. "One . . . two. . . ."

"Wait!" the Kubaz pleaded. "Do not kill me. I will not reveal where to find the young Hutt. But killing me will accomplish nothing. Let us both live, and perhaps in time you will become reconciled to your loss."

"Wrong answer, bug eater," Solo said, and began to

slowly squeeze the trigger, hoping that the sight would scare the Kubaz into talking.

There really wasn't any danger, because the blaster didn't work. Solo only kept it around as a prop for interrogations.

The Kubaz shook. Behind his dark lenses, Solo could see his eyes widen. "Wait!" he yelled, "Do not blast my face, human. I desire to continue my existence."

"Good," Solo said. "'Cause I sure didn't want to have to pay the cleaning bill for making a mess out of you. Now, where can I find Grubba?"

"My hive-mate has taken the young Hutt to our home world, Kubindi."

"Well, that narrows it down," Solo said. "What am I supposed to do, wander the whole planet? Give me specifics!" He jammed the blaster into the Kubaz's snout.

"Our hive mother is Queen Zabin. Our nest is near the Silver Forest of Dreams." The Kubaz crossed his paws before his chest in a protective gesture.

Behind Solo, Chewbacca growled a warning.

"Yeah, I know," Solo said. "We better get out of here." He looked around the cantina. An alien band was starting to play in the corner, and the bar was wreathed in so much smoke that Solo could hardly make out his friend Luke Skywalker, who was keeping watch for stormtroopers over by the door.

Luke gestured frantically. It had only been a matter of hours since Solo had blasted off from the old monastery outside Jabba's palace. By now, Jabba knew that Han Solo had lost Grubba. He was sure to be out for Solo's blood.

Solo pulled a robe over his head. He didn't like sneaking

around, but his face was well-known in these parts. In minutes, he was out of the cantina, and weaving through the busy streets of Mos Eisley.

"So you got the information?" Luke asked.

"Yeah, we're going to someplace called the Silver Forest of Dreams, on Kubindi."

"I've heard of that place," Luke said. "It's supposed to be strong in the Force."

"I've heard of Kubindi, too," Solo countered, "and I hear that they've got antz there that are so big, you can ride them like a speeder bike."

As they walked through a market filled with Jawa merchants, Luke bent his head in thought. "Something's wrong," he said suddenly. "I have a bad feeling about this. Maybe whoever took Grubba doesn't want the child at all. Maybe they want you! They could be using Grubba as the bait."

"Well, it's nice to be wanted," Solo joked. "And if Grubba's the bait, I'm biting. 'Cause when Jabba finds out that I lost his Ur-Damo, he's going to be one mad Hutt."

"We have to be careful," Luke said.

Chewie roared agreement.

"Well, you know me, kid. *Careful* is my middle name." With Luke and Chewie following, Solo hurried to the spaceport.

Someone must have spotted Solo at the cantina, because as he rounded a corner, he saw half a dozen local city militia rushing toward him. Luckily, they were trying to run through a bunch of Jawa traders, who blocked and distracted them.

"This way!" Luke shouted. He grabbed Solo's arm and pulled him into an alley, where a pair of banthas were munching leaf pellets. For a moment Solo, Luke, and Chewbacca all stood with their backs to the street, dumping moist pellets into the banthas' food bin. After the city guards had run past, Luke quickly turned and resumed walking.

At the spaceport, Princess Leia Organa and the droids See-Threepio and Artoo-Detoo waited inside the *Millennium Falcon.*

"We're going to Kubindi," Solo said as he entered the ship.

Leia gave him an odd look. "Not much is known about that planet. Lots of solar flares, and I hear the wildlife can be pretty rough."

"Solar flares, oh my!" See-Threepio groaned. The droid held both hands to his head. "I'm sure they'll wreak havoc on my circuitry." Artoo-Detoo gave a little electronic squeal of agreement.

"Yeah, the flares might have you bumping into trees and falling into holes all right," Solo said. "But if I were you, I'd worry more about their beetuls. I hear they can dig through solid metal, and they love things that are nice and gold and shiny."

"Oh no!" Threepio exclaimed.

"Solo, don't tease the droids," Leia said.

"Whatever you say, princess. But I'm not teasing."

"Princess Leia," Threepio said, "might I suggest that we fill the cargo hold with some universal insecticides?"

"Not a bad idea," Solo said. "I'll buy us each a giant fliswatter, too." At that moment, he heard the *chug, chug, chug* of the *Falcon*'s auto-cannon begin to fire. "Unfortunately, we don't have time."

A monitor on the forward observation deck showed the door to the docking bay outside. A dozen local militia wearing tan and gray battle armor were sprinting into the docking bay. Chewbacca raced into the cockpit.

"Chewie, lock up the ship!" Solo shouted. "We're blasting out of here."

Solo ran for the pilot's seat, calling orders for the astrogation computer to calculate the jump to Kubindi. Luke and Leia buckled themselves in.

See-Threepio grabbed onto a table as the ship blasted off, shaking badly as the *Falcon* shot through the turbulence of the upper atmosphere.

"Oh I abhor space travel," he told Artoo. "I hope my innards are welded in tight. We weren't made for such abuse!"

Artoo whistled confidently in his mechanical voice.

"Well, all right. Maybe *you* were made for such abuse, but I'm sure I can hear my motivator clanging against something in my head."

Grubba the Hutt was playing sabacc with three bounty hunters in Dengar's ship, *Punishing One*. They sat in chairs bolted around a table.

"Ha, ha, ha," Grubba said in a voice that seemed far too deep for such a small creature. "I win again." He reached out his small paws and pulled the gambling chips toward him.

"You're cheating," Udin the Kubaz said, his voice translator conveying a threat in his tone.

"Prove it, and maybe I'll give some of the money back," Grubba offered. It was dreadfully hard to cheat at sabacc. It was impossible to know what the electronic cards would display until the card's button had been punched. It was possible to hot wire some of the circuitry to be given a good hand, but since the cards were shuffled between each turn, it made it almost impossible to hold a card from one hand to the next.

The three bounty hunters scowled over the table at Grubba. The young Hutt was cleaning them out. Surely, somehow, the child was cheating.

"I now own three-quarters interest in any reward my dear Ur-Damo Jabba pays for me." The young Hutt fixed each bounty hunter with a cold glare.

"I can't wait to get rid of you, worm-face," Eron Stonefield said. "You're more unbearable when you're winning sabacc than when you're losing."

The young Hutt licked his lips with an ugly purple tongue. "Aw, come on, Eron. Is that any way to talk to a Hutt who loves you? Give me a kiss, and I'll give your money back."

The gorgeous Eron Stonefield swept her red hair back with one hand. "Sorry, I never kiss anyone who leaves a slime trail."

"Why, that's half the men you know!" Grubba said. "Someday when I'm rich, I'm going to buy you and keep you for a slave."

"The way you play sabacc, you might own me by the end of the week," Eron groaned, throwing down her cards.

"I don't understand," Udin the Kubaz said. "You say that you were going to Jabba's so he could train you in the family business. But you already seem to know much about crime — or at least how to cheat at cards."

"My Ur-Damo Jabba is a specialist in the shipping

trade," Grubba explained. "My side of the family special-izes in gambling enterprises. I go to learn his trade."

"Shipping business?" Eron said. "That's a mild term. He's a smuggler."

"He is a shipper," Grubba countered. "He faces all the problems that legitimate shippers face — the need to get goods from the seller to the buyer, equipment malfunc-tions, the threat of space piracy, and the constant worries about competitors undercutting his price."

"But he's a smuggler," Eron repeated.

Dengar knew Hutts better than Eron did. "Hutts don't think like we do," he advised. "The Empire's laws don't concern Hutts."

"Exactly," Grubba agreed. "In trading unlawful mer-chandise, Jabba merely increases both his risks and his re-wards. He is a well-respected trader by Hutt standards."

"But he murders his competitors," Eron argued.

"If they stopped competing, he would not be forced to kill them," Grubba said.

"So he values money more than life." Eron shook her head. Decency and morality were concepts that some aliens would never understand. Certain species had evolved to be far more selfish and solitary than humans. Sitting in the same room with Grubba gave Eron the creeps. And the Kubaz was no better. Though Udin seemed to feel some affinity for humans and obeyed human laws, he also loved the taste of insects so much that he did not care whether his source of protein was dead or not. Some Kubaz eating habits bordered on cannibalism.

A proximity indicator began to beep as the ship dropped out of hyperspace. The ship's viewer showed a rich planet — expansive seas, violet forests, slashes of red desert.

Udin stared at the planet longingly, his gray trunk hanging limp. When he spoke, the translator pinned to his lapel said in reverent tones, "Ah, home on Kubindi, most beautiful of all worlds. I can almost taste its succulent wroches, its tender termytes! Here, my hive grows the plumpest and tastiest spydrs in the galaxy. Soon we will feast on delicacies you have never imagined!"

As the *Punishing One* flew low over Kubindi, Dengar marveled. It was a sweet land. Lush jungles, wide rivers, a few vast cities, and expansive farms. Yet only on close examination did one see how odd a world it was.

The Kubaz lived in cities, all right, but they were strange cities — their towers rose high from the ground, but the buildings and roads all looked as if they were a single piece of material, a dull gray in color. There were signs of technology — vehicles in landing bays, communications towers, and sensor dishes. Yet as Dengar flew over the cities, he saw almost no one.

Suddenly Dengar realized that the Kubaz lived primarily underground. What he had first thought to be towering buildings were actually enormous ventilation shafts. Dengar spotted movement near a shaft, and thought it would be Kubaz workers. Instead, a single Kubaz directed a herd of giant termytes as they built a new dome. The giant termytes were carrying gray pulp, chewing it, and then tamping it into place to form a sort of gray cement.

For as far as Dengar could see, he found fields for the strange crops and herds. In one field was an enormous farm for purple melons. In a field nearby, the melons were fed to iridescent blue beetuls as large as his spaceship. Each beetul had a trio of horns rising from its massive head.

In another field, a small Kubaz girl herded a flock of enormous green-and-yellow-striped fliis. Their wings were clipped, so they wouldn't take to the sky. Nearby, giant fire-red millipods wallowed in a bog.

Dengar had no words for many of the herds of over-sized insects — they were so unlike any that he had ever seen. Something huge, with skeletal limbs, had hauled its bloated gray sack of a belly up from a river. When it saw the spaceship flying low, it raced back into the water.

In other places, flocks of giant wingfliis were making a slow migration overhead, and the sunlight shining through their yellow and orange wings made it look like a ribbon of fire burning in the sky.

"A pretty enough place," Eron Stonefield said into Dengar's ear.

"But I've heard it's dangerous, once out in the wilds," Dengar said.

Soon they swept over the inhabited lands, toward the stark mountains. The prevailing vegetation had been lush, a dark violet in color. Now, ahead in the tall mountains, Dengar could see trees sparkling like cut glass in the sunlight. The Silver Forest of Dreams.

"Ah," Udin exulted, "my home lies near. We are a poor hive, as you see, and live far from the city. Our ghost spydrs are too deadly to raise close to town."

"What do you mean, deadly?" Grubba the Hutt asked with a smile, slithering close to the monitor.

"The ghost spydrs carry a deadly poison in their bite," Udin explained. "In my hive, when we are small, our mothers begin injecting the poison into our veins, so that we soon develop immunities. Still, as my guests, you must beware. The spydrs build enormous webs all through the woods near my hive, and also make trip-wires in the forest. You may go near them only at your peril."

From his pilot's seat, Dengar looked back at Udin with new respect. He had wondered why Udin insisted that the hive on his home world would be a good place to set an ambush. He'd thought only that Udin's kin would shield him from any reprisals that Solo or the Rebels might offer.

"So," Dengar asked, "you expect the spydrs to get Han Solo before we do?"

Udin nodded wisely. "Humans walking through the Silver Forest of Dreams could not possibly evade the spydrs. Some will surely die. It is a slow death, very painful."

"And your hive-mates will help us?" Dengar asked.

Udin wriggled his trunk, giving a Kubaz nod. "You shall see, soon enough."

At dusk the *Punishing One* entered the Silver Forest of Dreams. The trees rose thousands of yards high, and their upper branches wove together to form an impenetrable canopy.

Rising mists and vapor were trapped in the air. The ship flew through these mists, through the odd silver wood. Dengar turned on the landing lights, and everything in the wood glittered brilliantly in shades of silver — the silver trees, the silver mists.

Suddenly, in the fog, Dengar spotted a flock of enormous msqitos, each fully as long as a man, with an enormous wingspan. He banked hard right to avoid them and almost crashed into a tree. Quickly recovering, Dengar found himself weaving through the fog and thick branches.

He tried to slow down, but his sensors said the huge alien bugs were following him.

It was dangerous to fly in these swamps.

Dengar dropped altitude and lost the insects in the fog.

"Down so low," Udin said, "it is possible that your ship might be ensnared in the webs of ghost spydrs. The webs are as strong as steel, and very sticky. You would not want to get the ship entangled in one. Please fly higher."

Sweat ran from Dengar's brow. He nodded and nosed the ship higher.

A voice came over the ship's communicator. A Kubaz warned, "Pilot, you are in a danger zone. Please reverse course. To approach without assistance is impossible."

Udin said, "All hail Queen Zabin, leader of our great hive. It is I, Udin. I have returned!"

"Udin!" the voice on the communicator said. "Greetings. Have you finished spying on the humans? Have you brought some succulent new species for us to eat?"

"Uh, not exactly," Udin confessed. He flipped off his translator and began speaking rapidly in Kubaz.

Dengar halted the ship and let it hover for a moment. He studied the gray-skinned Udin. The creature, in hood and goggles, looked like a spy. Dengar didn't mind. Most species, when they first met the Empire, sent out some sort of scout or spy to study alien societies and customs, with the hope of gathering illicit technology. It was part of the process of getting to know your galactic neighbors. But he was worried by the fact that the Kubaz always seemed to be on the prowl for something to eat.

After awhile, Udin switched his translator back on. "Our gracious queen has agreed to harbor us, and to aid us in capturing the insane Rebels. You may release the controls to your ship. Tractor beams mounted in the trees will navigate us through."

Dengar sat back, letting the ship hover. The *Punishing One* lurched forward with a groan and began its journey toward the hive city of Queen Zabin.

It was a weird and wondrous journey, through the silver trees and the mists. The ship began to weave, pulled by tractor beams through tunnels. On every side Dengar could see the great sheets of web from ghost spydrs, and sometimes when the ship stirred the air the enormous spydrs would race out to watch.

The spydrs were as pale as fog and nearly as large as the ship. Their dark faceted eyes gleamed like onyx, and their legs were long and amazingly slender.

Seeing them gave Dengar a creepy feeling. He knew that without the aid of the Kubaz, he would never get out of the city alive.

By the time Dengar saw the enormous gray air shafts of the Kubaz's underground city rising up like skyscrapers amid a sunny clearing in the jungle, he almost felt sorry for Han Solo.

Udin had been right about this place. Solo would never make it to the Kubaz hive alive.

CHAPTER TWO

Luke Skywalker didn't like the looks of Kubindi. It wasn't just the fact that the locals raised insects for consumption, or the fact that Kubindi's sun was tremendously hot and kept emitting enormous solar flares.

It was the Silver Forest of Dreams. Even in childhood, he'd heard tales of the legendary place. The forest was said to be powerful in the Force. As they drew near, Luke saw the trees were as tall and stately as crystal. It seemed beautiful and pleasant. But there was a power here — a dark power.

The *Millennium Falcon* skirted the edge of the forest. As Solo began to fly in, Luke reached out a hand to stop him. "Don't go in there, Han. That's what they want us to do."

Solo and Chewbacca looked up at Luke from their pilot seats. Leia and the droids stood behind Luke in the cockpit.

"What are you talking about, kid?" Solo asked. "I can fly through just about anything."

"I trust your piloting skills," Luke said. "But this might be a trap you're flying into. I don't know . . . I dreamt about it last night. I saw . . . webs. The ship swallowed in webs, and something enormous coming to get us." Luke had wakened abruptly from this nightmare. He'd thrown off his blankets, unable to sleep anymore.

"Listen to him," Leia advised. "I . . . have a spooky feeling about this place, too."

"What, are you afraid of a little spydr, Princess?"

"We'll sneak in quietly, on the ground," Luke said. "It is the only way."

"We don't even know where their city is!" Solo protested. "It might be a long walk in that forest."

"Look, a town!" See-Threepio proclaimed.

Luke looked at the monitors and saw the tall gray spires of a nearby village, not far from the forest's edge. "Maybe we can rent vehicles there," he said.

A meandering highway led to the village through the hills, then disappeared into the distance. The Kubaz village was sheltered beneath a few feet of something that looked like concrete. The upper levels of the city contained some Kubaz inns and restaurants.

As Luke entered the subterranean village with the droids and the others, rich smells of exotic foods greeted him. The smell came from a stall where a vendor sold roasted bugs. The vendor, an old Kubaz woman with a long wrinkled trunk, pulled out a worn, hand-held translator. "You like? These Silver Forest rootrubs are our specialty."

One taste of the rich, spicy meat convinced Luke. He bought enough for Leia, Solo, and Chewbacca.

As he approached the knot of others, See-Threepio rushed up to him. "Sir," the droid said, "I've done some preliminary calculations on the bio-mass of the Silver Forest. The trees there should give me excellent protection from any solar flares. I'll be able to come with you!"

"That's great, Threepio," Luke said. "I'm sure your sensors will come in handy."

"Oh, I'll be invaluable!" See-Threepio agreed.

Luke hurried past the droid. Solo was speaking to a guide, a Kubaz named Bizzin Uz who was taller and stronger than any Kubaz Luke had ever seen. The guide was used to wilderness travel and was displaying his vehicles — little two-man landspeeders similar to the one Luke had owned on Tatooine. Each speeder had communications consoles and a heavy blaster mounted to the dash.

"The speeders look good," Han said. "Can you take us there?"

"Why do you want to go?" the guide asked. "The hive of Queen Zabin is deep in the forest. The journey is dangerous. And those in her hive are not to be trusted. They protect the forest from intruders."

"Yeah," Solo answered, "well let's just say I've got some personal business there, and I'm pretty dangerous myself. Can you take me? What will it cost?"

"I will take you," the guide answered. "But the cost will be high."

"How high?"

The Kubaz paused, then looked directly at Solo. "Maybe your life."

MISSION BRIEFING

Before you proceed, you must consult the Mission Guide for the rules of the STAR WARS MISSIONS. You must follow these rules at all times.

This is a Rebel mission.

Han Solo is trying to rescue Grubba the Hutt from bounty hunters on the planet Kubindi. You and your fellow Rebels are in a Kubindi city on the outskirts of the Silver Forest of Dreams. A guide has agreed to lead you into the forest, where giant deadly insects run rampant. Once you get there, your job is to enter the hive of Queen Zabin and rescue the young Hutt.

You may take any weapons you want. On this Mission, you may use Power three times. Your guide has provided you with a modified landspeeder.

You start the mission with your MP total from your previous mission. (Or 1000 MP, if this is your first Mission.)

Choose your character now.

May the Force be with you!

Your Mission: The Search for Grubba the Hutt

Near dark, when the danger of solar flares has lessened, Bizzin Uz asks you to climb into the landspeeders.

Each Rebel will be accompanied by a droid. You will take See-Threepio in the back of your speeder.

Bizzin Uz says to all of you, "Whatever you do, don't slow down. The insects will swarm all over you. Your head-lights will blind any bugs in front of you, and you can use the heavy blaster to clear them out of the way.

"Oh — and if you see any Kubaz in the forest, escape quick. They're either poachers or police from the Zabin hive. In either case, they will try to kill you."

The landspeeder bounces around as you and See-Threepio settle into the seat. The repulsor-lift field holds it off the ground. The twin turbine engines whine as you power up.

Bizzin Uz leads you up the winding highway toward the forest. You see the day's hatch of giant msqitos flying in a great cloud from a lake toward the trees. You shudder.

Suddenly Bizzin Uz veers from the road and heads out over the lake. The other landspeeders kick up a wake in front of you, splattering it against the Duraplex windscreen of your speeder. Some lake water gets in your mouth. It tastes salty.

"Pardon me," See-Threepio says, "but this water is very corrosive. I wouldn't want to damage my circuits."

"Okay," you say, and you whip to the right, so that you're no longer driving on anyone's tail.

You see a giant msqito, as long as a man, come dipping toward the water a hundred yards ahead of you and just to your right. Suddenly, the water crests, and an enormous water monster leaps after the msqito.

A water monster the size of a whale!

The waves from the monster come crashing toward your landspeeder. If they hit, the landspeeder will flip and be swamped.

To avoid the waves: Add your strength# to your skill# +3 for your confront#. Roll the 12-dice to steer through the waves.

If your confront# is equal to or more than your roll#, add the difference to your MP total. You have managed to buck the waves. You may proceed.

If your confront# is lower than your roll#, subtract the difference from your MP total. Add +2 to your confront# for your new confront#. Roll the 12-dice again and repeat this confront with your new confront# until you steer past the waves.

Over the communicator, Bizzin Uz shouts, "Watch out! Flip off your headlights, or that creature will have you next!"

You flip off your headlights — too late! The water just ahead is bubbling as something enormous prepares to snap at you. You see the fin and back of an enormous water monster.

You may fight the giant water monster (using your own weapon or your vehicle's heavy blasters), you may dodge the water monster, or you may try to block the water monster (using Power).

To fight the giant water monster (using your own weapon): Choose your weapon. Add your weaponry# to your weapon's far-range# +3 for your confront#. Roll the 12-dice to shoot the water monster.

If your confront# is equal to or more than your roll#, add the difference +4 to your MP total. It's a perfect hit. The monster dives away, looking for a gentler meal, and you may now proceed.

If your confront# is lower than your roll#, subtract the difference from your MP total. At the speed you're going, you only had time for one shot. Now you must dodge or block the monster, or use your vehicle's weapon (below).

To fight the water monster (using your vehicle's weapon): Add your weaponry# to your vehicle's weapon# +4 for your confront#. Roll the 12-dice to fire the laser cannon.

If your confront# is equal to or more than your roll#, add the difference +5 to your MP total. You've scored a direct hit and may now proceed.

If your confront# is lower than your roll#, subtract the difference from your MP total. At the speed you're going, you only had time for one shot. Now you must dodge or block the monster (below).

To dodge the water monster: Your stealth# +1 is your confront#. Roll the 6-dice to dodge the monster.

If your confront# is equal to or more than your roll#, add the difference +3 to your MP total. You deftly sweep past the beast. You may now proceed.

If your confront# is lower than your roll#, subtract the difference from your MP total. You slowed your vehicle and tried to circle, but the beast is after you. Now you hit the thrusters and surge forward. Add +2 to your confront# for your new confront#. Roll again to dodge the fish, using the new confront#. Continue doing this until you have escaped from the water monster.

To block the water monster (using Power)*: Choose your Object Movement Power. Your skill# + your Power's mid-resist# + your Jedi# is your confront#. You try to maneuver a floating dead tree trunk into the monster's path. Roll the 6-dice to see if this works.

If your confront# is equal to or more than your roll#, add the difference +3 to your MP total. You wallop the beast and may proceed.

If your confront# is lower than your roll#, subtract the difference from your MP total. The trunk misses the beast. Now you must either fight (if you have not already fought) or dodge the fish (above).

*Note: This counts as one of three Power uses you are allowed on this Mission.

You escape the water monster, but suddenly Bizzin Uz and the others veer toward you. There wasn't just one creature. You've driven into a school of them!

Everyone ahead is speeding up, trying to outrace the monsters. Bizzin Uz veers sharply from an enormous water beast in front of him and nearly crashes into your speeder.

"Oh dear!" See-Threepio cries. "My sensors indicate that we're heading into real trouble!"

In the darkness, hovering over the water just ahead, you see enormous insects with long lacy wings — like giant green mayfliis. You flip on your headlights to warn the others, and are amazed.

The water ahead is filled by hundreds of these giant insects, all hovering low, dipping their tails into the water to deposit their eggs.

You can't slow down with the water monsters behind you. And you don't want to speed up — not when you're going to run into those insects.

As you drive into the giant fliis, you begin to swerve, veering past the creatures. You look at one, with its enormous faceted eyes reflecting your headlights, and its massive mandibles clacking. The chitin on its body looks as thick as the battle armor on an AT-AT. Its six enormous legs are big enough to crush your speeder.

The fliis are blinded by your headlights, unsure whether to evade or attack. The beating of their wings makes the water around them choppy.

To your left, other speeders begin to fire their weapons. Perhaps the noise will drive the beasts to a higher altitude. Or perhaps they are shooting the monsters.

Ahead of you, the giant fliis are an almost solid mass. Bizzin Uz sees that you have a good path, and he swerves ahead of you. Water sprays in your face as his craft raises a wake. This doesn't help!

"Look out!" Threepio cries as a giant fli buzzes in front to you.

You must shoot at a giant fli while veering to evade others.

To avoid the fli: Your weaponry# + your weapon's far-range# + your skill# + your vehicle's stealth# is your confront#. Roll the 12-dice to simultaneously drive and combat the giant fli.

> *If your confront# is equal to or more than your roll#,* add 10 MP to your MP total. The giant fli will now only bother you in your nightmares. You may proceed.

> *If your confront# is lower than your roll#,* subtract the difference from your MP total and repeat this confront until you have escaped the giant fli.

"Help!" Threepio shouts.

You look back to see an angry fli racing toward you from behind. Its enormous mandibles clack as it reaches forward to grab Threepio. The forward gun on the landspeeder won't do you any good! And the fliis are so thick ahead, there's no way to avoid them.

You can fight the giant fli with a weapon, or you can seek to hypnotize the fli with Power.

To combat the giant fli with a weapon: Choose your weapon. Add your weaponry# + your weapon's mid-range# +2 for your confront #. Roll the 12-dice.

> *If your confront# is equal to or more than your roll#,* add the difference to your MP total. Now that bug knows

what it's like to get slapped by a giant fliswatter! You may keep driving.

If your confront# is lower than your roll#, subtract the difference from your MP total. Add +2 to your confront# for your new confront#. Roll the 12-dice and continue this confront, using the new confront#, until the bug is nothing but water monster bait.

To hypnotize the fli (with Power)*: Choose your Hypnotism Power. Your Jedi# + your Power's low-resist# +2 is your confront#. Roll the 6-dice.

If your confront# is equal to or more than your roll#, add the difference to your MP total. The fli suddenly becomes subdued and looks for less violent diversion elsewhere. You may proceed.

If your confront# is lower than your roll#, subtract the difference from your MP total. The fli resists. You must fight (above).

*Note: This counts as one of three Power uses you are allowed on this Mission.

As you leave the flock of fliis behind, you hear the sound of water monsters leaping up from the water. You look back, and see the whale-sized aquabeast gulping down giant fliis. Your heart pounds in terror and you wipe sweat and saltwater spray from your forehead and eyes.

"Don't slow down!" Threepio warns.

In moments you reach the shore, near the Silver Forest of Dreams.

You drive into the great wood, and your headlights shine into the dank forest. A carpet of yellow fungus grows thick on the forest floor. Its long sticklike growths are as tall as your waist.

The landspeeders don't fly *over* it as much as they fly *through* it.

The trees themselves are enormous. At the base of the trunk, each silver tree is perhaps a hundred meters wide; from where you sit, you can't begin to see how tall they are. The speeders' headlights gleam off their silver bark, providing you with a strong light.

In the distance, grazing in the deep fungus, you see enormous beetuls — each the size of a landspeeder! They come in many colors, and some of them have enormous horns, like giant thorns sticking up from between their eyes. You imagine these beetuls rushing forward and ramming a vehicle. The thought gives you the chills.

It is no wonder that Bizzin Uz wanted you to drive a fast vehicle. Everywhere, there are signs of giant insects — from trails trampled through the fungus, to an enormous exposed root that has been chewed down to nothing.

You turn to a clump of blue rocks and are surprised when it suddenly moves. They're not rocks at all — they're giant mytes!

Mists and vapors hang in the air like a gauzy ceiling. You stare up, and never in your life have you felt quite so small. The wildlife, the silver woods, all suddenly seem beautiful, peaceful . . . and overwhelming.

You slow a moment to look at a tree. Something on the silver trunk glitters like rubies. You look closer and recognize dozens of fiery beetuls, each the size of your fist, climbing upward.

As you slow, something enormous and black slaps down at you. Whap!

It's the tail of a giant insect. It slams into the communications console of your landspeeder, and the console explodes in a flash of sparks and dark smoke. The tail wriggles, pumping vicious-looking poison into the console. The landspeeder slues sideways, and two giant black claws grab the speeder, tipping it sideways. You are afraid to look beneath you, but you do so anyway. It's a giant four-clawed scarpyen!

And it is firmly gripping the speeder.

"Oh dear!" See-Threepio cries. "We should never have slowed down."

As you realize the danger, you see the other speeders whizzing ahead, unaware of your plight.

A giant black claw reaches up to grab you. You can evade the claw (with Power), evade (without Power), or fight. Choose now.

To evade (with Power)*: Choose your Evasion Power. Your stealth# + your Jedi# + your Power's low-resist# is your confront#. Roll the 6-dice.

> If your confront# is equal to or more than your roll#, add 9 MP to your MP total. The claw gropes in the air, safely above you. You may proceed.

If your confront# is lower than your roll#, subtract the difference from your MP total. It didn't work. The claw grabs your arm, and you must fight (below).

*Note: This counts as one of three Power uses you are allowed on this Mission.

To evade (without Power): Your stealth# +1 is your confront#. Roll the 6-dice to evade the claw.

If your confront# is equal to or more than your roll#, add the difference +4 to your MP total. You deftly duck beneath the claw and may now get back to business.

If your confront# is lower than your roll#, subtract the difference from your MP total. The claw grasps your arm lightly, and you must fight (below).

To fight the scarpyen: Choose your weapon. Add your weaponry# to your weapon's close-range# for your confront#. Roll the 6-dice.

If your confront# is equal to or more than your roll#, add the difference +3 to your MP total. The monster won't ever crack nuts with that claw again!

If your confront# is lower than your roll#, subtract the difference from your MP total and repeat this confront. Add +2 to your confront# for your new confront#. Roll the 6-dice and repeat the confront, using the new confront#, until you defeat the claw.

With the claw out of the way, you glance over the side of the landspeeder. The monster is there in the fungus, lashing madly. It's getting ready to strike with its deadly tail. It is grasping with its claws. You've got to put it out of commission quickly!

You can fight the creature with or without Power. Or you can attempt to put the creature to sleep using Power.

To fight (with Power)*: Choose your weapon, and your Object Movement Power. You must smash the scarpyen with a tree trunk — *as* you fire your weapon. Add your weaponry# + your weapon's close-range# + your Jedi# + your Power's low-resist# +2 for your confront#. Roll the 12-dice to shoot the giant scarpyen.

If your confront# is equal to or more than your roll#, add 15 MP to your MP total. Bug parts fly everywhere. You may now proceed.

If your confront# is lower than your roll#, subtract the difference from your MP total. Add +2 to your confront# for your new confront#. Roll the 12-dice and repeat this confront until you have eliminated the creature.

*Note: This counts as one of three Power uses you are allowed on this Mission.

To combat the giant scarpyen (without Power): Choose your weapon. Add your weaponry# to your weapon's close-range# +3 for your confront#. Roll the 12-dice to shoot the scarpyen.

If your confront# is equal to or more than your roll#, add the difference +7 to your MP total. That's one messed-up bug. You may now drive off to look for your friends.

If your confront# is lower than your roll#, subtract the difference from your MP total. Add +3 to your confront# for your new confront#. Roll the 12-dice and repeat this confront, using the new confront#, until you have eliminated the creature.

To put the scarpyen to sleep (with Power)*: Choose your Sleep Power. Your Jedi# + your Power's low-resist# +2 is your confront#. Roll the 6-dice.

If your confront# is equal to or more than your roll#, add the difference +6 to your MP total. Now get out of there quick — who knows how long the monster will sleep?

If your confront# is lower than your roll#, subtract the difference from your MP total. It didn't work. The monster is about to rip up your landspeeder. You must fight (above).

*Note: This counts as one of three Power uses you are allowed on this Mission.

That wasn't easy. Reward yourself with 25 MP (45 MP for Advanced Level players).

You escape the scarpyen, but your friends are now far ahead. You can't see their headlights, and your communications console is a mess. You could try to fix it, but the gross blob of poison sitting on the dash convinces you otherwise.

Luckily you know the general direction the other speeders were heading in, so you flip on the headlights and speed away.

For a long time, your trip is fairly quiet. You don't spot any sign of the others, but everywhere there are wondrous insects.

In the deep of the forest, you come across an army of giant silver antz. Their warriors carry shields made of wood and bear axes made of crude stone. They wear thick armor made of woven moss, and have helmets that cover most of their heads. They stand almost upright, like humans. You're surprised to find that some of the insects here on Kubindi have developed such high intelligence. Their army has perhaps ten thousand members, marching across the forest floor, and they are cutting a swath of destruction everywhere they go — harvesting other insects, fungus, and roots.

You steer clear of them, even though this throws you off your intended course. There's still no sign of the others.

"Threepio," you sigh, "I think we're really lost. Can you help us find our way back to the *Falcon*?"

"I think so," Threepio reports. Then he suddenly taps you on the shoulder. "Look! We're saved!"

You see dim lights far ahead in the forest.

You race toward them. The lights bob up and down, and you wonder at their color, for they are more of a pale blue than the white of a landspeeder's lamplight.

You slow a bit, uncertain as you approach. Suddenly you see the source of the lights: Four giant fyrefliis are bobbing up and down in the woods.

"Oh, dear," See-Threepio says. "Those are no help."

You shake your head in defeat and turn the vehicle in a long, lazy arc.

Suddenly there is a loud clacking noise above, and Threepio shouts, "Aaaagh!"

You look up just as an enormous flying insect strikes. You catch a glimpse of it — a fierce white face, almost like a skull, with enormous black eyes. Giant legs are poised to strike. You reach for your weapon, but the insect grabs you with two strong pincers. Four legs wrap around your body, holding you like a vise.

As it lifts you in the air, Threepio shouts, "What shall I do?"

"Help!" you yell as the insect lifts you high into the air. Already you're two hundred meters aboveground, and climbing. You try to grasp your weapon. But if you kill the insect now, you'll fall to your death!

The insect climbs higher and higher, flying over a thousand meters into the air. The silver trunks of the great trees are like pillars in the darkness, and soon the lamplight from your landspeeder is so distant, it seems like a single star, far below.

Then the monster heads north, and you lose sight of the vehicle altogether.

You are apparently the captive of a giant mantys-like creature. You look at the way that its huge front pincers fold toward its belly, and realize that if it wanted, it could eat you as it flies. But the insect seems to have other plans.

It wants to stop and eat you somewhere private.

Quietly, you struggle in its grasp, and try to draw your weapon. It's not easy. You fear that if you wriggle too much, it will attract the beast's attention.

You can either retrieve your weapon with Power or without Power.

To draw your weapon (using Power)*: Choose your Object Movement Power. Your skill# + your Power's mid-resist# + your Jedi# is your confront#. Roll the 6-dice.

If your confront# is equal to or more than your roll#, add the difference to your MP total. Your weapon is firmly in your hand.

If your confront# is lower than your roll#, subtract the difference from your MP total. Repeat this confront until you retrieve your weapon, then proceed.

*Note: This counts as one of three Power uses you are allowed on this Mission.

To draw the weapon (without Power): Your stealth# +2 is your confront#. Roll the 6-dice to draw your weapon.

If your confront# is equal to or more than your roll#, add the difference +1 to your MP total. The weapon quietly slips into your hand.

If your confront# is lower than your roll#, subtract the difference from your MP total. You miss your weapon, but can always try again. Repeat this confront using the same confront# until you retrieve the weapon, and then proceed.

The insect carries you high into the woven branches of the tree, then drops into a nest of twigs and limbs and moss. The nest is full of grisly things — the skulls and bones of a dozen Kubaz, along with an old speeder bike, other pieces of metal, and the discarded shells of dead bugs.

As soon as the insect's feet touch the nest, you roll to the side. You must fight.

To combat the giant insect: Choose your weapon. Add your weaponry# to your weapon's close-range# +4 for your confront#. Roll the 12-dice to shoot the creature.

If your confront# is equal to or more than your roll#, add the difference to your MP total. The beast is blown over the edge of the nest — you may now proceed.

If your confront# is lower than your roll#, subtract the difference from your MP total. Add +2 to your confront# for your new confront#. Roll the 12-dice and repeat this confront, using your new confront#, until you have wasted the beast.

That bug will never try to eat a Rebel again. Reward yourself 17 MP (27 for Advanced Level players).

You begin searching the nest, hoping to find a parachute or something.

You find an old speeder bike that has been fiercely crushed. It is useless . . . except for a battered pack you see on it. You open the pack. Inside is some rotten food and a BlasTech DH-17 blaster pistol — a perfect weapon for fighting giant bugs, since it can blow big holes in their hard outer shells. Add the weapon to your arsenal.

You also find a little hand-lantern, along with a knife, and some ultra-thin towing cable. The rest of the stuff is just junk — comic books written in Kubaz, some Kubaz snout ornaments, and clothes that won't fit you.

You poke around, looking among the bones of insects and Kubaz, but find nothing more that will be helpful.

You look down, but can no longer see the lights of the landspeeder. You call for help, but See-Threepio doesn't answer. The mantys didn't just carry you straight up, it carried you north.

You ponder your predicament, and decide that you can either starve to death up here or fall to your death while trying to climb down the tree.

Falling seems faster.

You walk along a twisted limb, which is about as thick as your waist. The bark of the silver tree feels rubbery under your feet. The tree sways gently in the night wind, and you're almost grateful that you can't see how far you will fall if you trip. You are acutely conscious of the fact that if you do slip, you'll have to grab onto the limb.

Everywhere above, you hear the sound of wind rushing through leaves.

A gust blows, and the limb suddenly sways beneath your feet.

To avoid falling: Add your strength# to your skill# +3, for your confront#. Roll the 12-dice.

If your confront# is equal to or more than your roll#, add the difference +6 to your MP total. You easily stay on the limb. You may proceed.

If your confront# is lower than your roll#, subtract the difference from your MP total. You fall over, and must grasp the branch and climb back up (below).

To climb back up the branch (if you have fallen): Your strength# + your skill# is your confront#. Roll the 6-dice to grasp the branch.

If your confront# is equal to or more than your roll#, add the difference to your MP total. You drag yourself up onto the branch. You may proceed.

If your confront# is lower than your roll#, subtract the difference from your MP total. You fall farther back. You must reach for the branch again (below).

To reach for the branch: Your strength# +1 is your confront#. Roll the 6-dice to get a proper hold.

If your confront# is equal to or more than your roll#, add the difference to your MP total. You have the branch in reach. Now you must climb back up (above).

If your confront# is lower than your roll#, subtract the difference from your MP total. You must try again, using the same confront equation.

You reach the base of the limb. Even here, the trunk of the tree looks as if it is seventy meters across. As you search the trunk for handholds, you realize that trying to climb down the smooth trunk would be nearly impossible.

Reluctantly, you pull out the towing cable and tie it around the tree limb. The cable is remarkably thin and strong. As you unroll it, you find that it is perhaps five hundred meters long.

You know that you're much higher in the tree than that. But you reason that at least you'll get down lower, and maybe then Threepio will be able to hear your shouts for help. Or maybe you can flash your light around, so that someone below will know that you're stuck.

You take the rope and put it between your legs, then pull some of it up and wrap it over your shoulder. The friction of the rope coiled around your body will keep you from falling too fast. This is called *body rappelling*, and is just one skill that every Rebel soldier must learn. It's not the safest way to climb down a giant tree, but as long as you're careful and don't twist the ropes, you should be all right.

You drop off the limb and begin rappelling down the tree. Soon you're sweating from the exertion. You slow down. Two hundred meters farther, you find another tree limb. You kick against the trunk of the tree and swing over to it so that you can rest.

There's still no sign of See-Threepio.

You rappel down farther. A hundred meters. Two hundred and fifty. You find what looks to be a huge cave, so you stop for a second and flash your light inside.

Some kind of huge gnawing insect has been eating the tree. There is rough sawdust all around the burrow. You shine the light in, but can't see any bug.

You swing into the burrow for a breather.

You shine your light down, and see that there isn't much towing cable left — fifty meters at the most. It's not enough to get to the next branch.

You take your weapon and fire once, cutting the cable. You roll it up, thinking it might come in handy later on.

With your light leading the way, you creep into the core of the burrow.

Instead of finding just one cave, you discover a maze of tunnels where the digging creature — or creatures — have burrowed. The tunnels go off in all directions — winding around in curlicues, dropping down what seems like ten meters in one spot, then climbing ten meters the next. The tunnels look very old. The pulp of the wood on the floors is dry and moldy. In some places, you unearth plodding mytes as large as your head. They flee at the sight of your little flashlight.

You choose a tunnel and follow it through, always searching for paths that lead down.

For a long hour you descend. As you do, you realize that the tunnel is getting wider and wider. The signs of digging look fresher. Whatever is chewing into the tree has been doing it for years. And it is growing. You could easily fly a landspeeder through these caverns.

You move farther, until you smell a putrid odor — the stench of rancid fat. It grows stronger and stronger.

The cave widens even more. At one point, it intersects

again with the outside. You step into the fresh air, and shine your light down. Dimly, you think you can see the ground. Maybe five hundred meters down. You wonder if you could climb for it. But it's an enormous drop. Still, the folds in the bark are deeper, giving you a hand-hold. And lichens grow in patches on the bark down here — thick bushlike plants that you *might* be able to hang onto.

No, you decide. It's still too risky to climb.

You go back into the cave and head farther down its twisted way. There is a noise in the cave now. The cracking and tearing of giant mandibles as they rip wood from the tree. The low rumble of the creature as it grinds its food with enormous teeth.

You wonder what could be down here. A giant bug? A beetul?

What will it do if it sees your light?

You really don't want to confront the creature, but there seems to be only one way down.

You draw nearer to the noise, as the cavern grows wider and wider still. The beast is not far.

You turn a corner and flash your light ahead.

The terror that confronts you is like nothing you've ever imagined. An enormous creature, a giant termyte, turns to glare at you. Its body is a milky pale color. Its small eyes are like clusters of emerald. Its mandibles are large enough to crush an armored vehicle.

The beast shrieks a strange, otherworldly cry, and lurches in your direction.

You must evade the creature with Power, evade without Power, or fight. Choose now.

To evade (with Power)*: Choose your Evasion Power. Your stealth# + your Jedi# + your Power's mid-resist# is your confront#. Roll the 6-dice.

If your confront# is equal to or more than your roll#, add the difference +7 to your MP total. The huge bug glances your way, then turns back to eating. You may proceed.

If your confront# is lower than your roll#, subtract the difference from your MP total. It didn't work. The megamuncher charges toward you, and you must fight (below).

*Note: This counts as one of three Power uses you are allowed on this Mission.

To evade without Power: Your stealth# +2 is your confront#. Roll the 6-dice to evade the lethal insect.

If your confront# is equal to or more than your roll#, add the difference +9 to your MP total. You quickly and quietly slip back up the burrow.

If your confront# is lower than your roll#, subtract the difference from your MP total. The huge bug lunges for you, and you must battle it (below).

To fight the monster: Choose your weapon. Add your weaponry# to your weapon's mid-range# for your confront#. Roll the 6-dice.

If your confront# is equal to or more than your roll#, add the difference +5 to your MP total. Wouldn't it be great to mount that bug's head on your wall back home!

If your confront# is lower than your roll#, subtract the difference from your MP total and repeat this confront until you defeat the bug.

Whew, do you ever feel like bug bait. Add 30 MP to your MP total (40 for Advanced Level players).

With the terror out of the way, you climb back up to the lowest exit, and look down once more. It's a long way down, and there's no way you're going to try that climb in the dark.

You are lower now than you've ever been. You lie down in the nice soft sawdust on the floor of the cave, and try to sleep.

In the night, you dream of trees. You dream of being a great silver tree, with your limbs fluttering beneath the green moonlight of Kubindi's triple moons. In the dream, you feel the contentment of being a tree, of feeling no wants, of tasting the fresh air in your leaves.

It seems a good life, a peaceful life, to be a tree.

And yet you also feel the pain of it. You feel the insects in your branches, tearing at your leaves. You feel the many termytes boring their way through your body. And you can do nothing about it.

At your base is a giant white spydr.

You wake up sweating, and you wonder if the tree in which you sit has been trying to speak to you in your dreams. On some worlds, such plants have been found — even plants that are wise or strong in the Force.

Does the tree want you to avenge it, or to protect it from the giant termytes? Does it want to thank you for killing the insects around it?

Or was this strange dream brought about merely by the many odd sights and sounds of this day?

You see that dawn is breaking.

Distantly, you hear Threepio call, "Help! Help! Can anyone hear me?"

"Threepio?!" you shout. "Up here!" You pull out your little light and shine it into the forest.

In moments, the droid comes around with the landspeeder. He is wrestling with the controls — like most droids, See-Threepio would easily fail a landspeeder driver's test. Still, he comes within view. But he cannot make it up to your height.

"There you are! Oh, I'm so glad you're alive!"

"Me too!" you say. "Help me get down from here."

"I'm afraid I'm not much good at climbing," Threepio laments.

"Look around," you say. "Maybe you could pile up some leaves or something, in case I fall."

Threepio scouts around for a moment, circles part of the tree.

"Good news!" he shouts. "There is a large spydrweb down here near the base of the tree. It would make a fine safety net! If you jump into that, it should protect you adequately."

"Is there a spydr in it?" you ask.

"Not at the moment," Threepio shouts.

You look down to where Threepio is pointing. You can't see any spydrweb. But you decide it wouldn't be a very useful web it you could see it.

You climb out onto the tree trunk, scrabbling for a hold. The thick lichen grows like small gray bushes here, but when you grab it, it feels brittle.

You circle the tree a bit, climbing down as you go. Suddenly, the lichens snap in your hand —

You're falling!

You must kick away from the tree, so that you won't get scraped up as you fall.

To kick away from the tree: your strength# +1 is your confront#. Roll the 6-dice.

If your confront# is equal to or more than your roll#, add the difference +2 to your MP total. You clear the tree.

If your confront# is lower than your roll#, subtract 7 MP from your MP total. You got scraped up in the fall.

As you fall, you try to draw your weapon, just in case there is a spydr in the web.

To draw your weapon, your skill# +2 is your confront#. Roll the 6-dice.

If your confront# is equal to or more than your roll#, add the difference to your MP total. You have your weapon in hand.

If your confront# is lower than your roll#, subtract the difference from your MP total. You manage to grasp your weapon, but you also sprain your wrist in the fall. Subtract 1 from your skill# for the remainder of this adventure.

You land in the web, and it lets you bounce within it, like a trampoline. But it's also sticky, and grips you tight.

You struggle to hold your weapon. You look to the ground. As the web stops bouncing, you feel it jiggle slightly, and look up. Near the top of the web, a small hole has been gnawed into the tree.

An enormous white spydr is there, pale as a ghost. It looks at you with dark, faceted eyes. Its mandibles are dripping orange poison.

On enormous slender legs, it stalks toward you in a delicate dance.

It's what you feared — a ghost spydr.

You may fight it, escape the web with Power, or escape without Power.

To escape (with Power)*: Choose your Evasion Power or your Object Movement Power. Your stealth# + your Jedi# + your Power's mid-resist# is your confront#. Roll the 6-dice.

If your confront# is equal to or more than your roll#, add the difference +11 to your MP total. Then drop gently from the web to the ground. You may proceed.

If your confront# is lower than your roll#, subtract the difference from your MP total. It didn't work. The spyder dances toward you, and you must fight (below).

*Note: This counts as one of three Power uses you are allowed on this Mission.

To escape (without Power): Your stealth# + your strength# is your confront#. Roll the 6-dice.

If your confront# is equal to or more than your roll#, add the difference +14 to your MP total. You deftly leap from the web.

If your confront# is lower than your roll#, subtract the difference from your MP total. The spydr leaps at you, and you must battle it (below).

To fight the spider: Add your weaponry# to your weapon's mid-range# for your confront#. Roll the 6-dice.

If your confront# is equal to or more than your roll#, add the difference +8 to your MP total. The spydr is now dangling from its own web.

If your confront# is less than your roll#, subtract the difference from your MP total and repeat this confront. Add +2 to your confront# for your new confront#. Repeat the confront, using the new confront#, until the spydr is dead.

You hop into the landspeeder and take one last look up into the giant tree. A moment later, a voice whispers through the air, "Protect the trees."

You drive off in the landspeeder, plowing through fields of ropy yellow fungus. The sunshine does not reach so far down in the forest, but the silver trees reflect the light, so the forest glows up above.

See-Threepio is clearly relieved that you are behind the wheel again. As you drive, you come across a trail in the woods. Three other landspeeders have been through here recently, and you realize that you have found the path left by the others. You follow it for a mile or so, and find signs of disaster.

Two of the landspeeders hit a spydrweb in the dark, and ran up high into it.

The landspeeders are caught in the web, and all around are signs that several other landspeeders drove here afterward. Six dead ghost spydrs cling to the sides of the web.

You look up, and see Bizzin Uz wrapped tightly in the webs. He is slowly twisting in the wind. The Kubaz opens his eyes weakly, and groans in pain.

"Leave me," he whispers. "I'm dying . . . Spydr bit me."

"I can get you to a doctor," you offer. "Surely there must be some way I can help."

"Too late . . ." the guide groans, and he coughs faintly.

"Where are my friends?"

"Captured. . . ." Bizzin Uz whispers. "Kubaz from Zabin's hive caught them. They think we are poachers. You must save them. . . ."

Bizzin Uz gasps softly. You get a canteen from the landspeeder and give him one last drink.

He opens his eyes. "Thank you," the Kubaz whispers. "Are you still here? Get away. The Zabins will return . . . to harvest the dead spydrs. . . ."

He begins struggling for breath. You try to help, but it's too late.

"Poor creature!" See-Threepio cries.

You look at Bizzin Uz's body, and decide to cut him down. But as you work, you suddenly hear the whirring sound of landspeeders coming toward you.

"We're doomed!" Threepio proclaims. He runs away from the tree in a blind panic.

"Quick," you say. "Get down. Hide!"

See-Threepio runs a few yards, then falls down in the tall fungus. His golden body gleams dully, but he's pretty well hidden. If he's lucky, he won't get caught. You, too, dive in.

Six landspeeders come roaring up, carrying a dozen fierce Kubaz warriors. Each wears body armor and carries a blaster rifle. Behind one landspeeder is a long, repulsor-lift sled for hauling the dead spydrs. The sled pulls up within a few feet of your hiding spot.

The Kubaz warriors step down from their vehicles and circle your landspeeder. They seem surprised to have found an extra vehicle and they look all around for signs of its occupants. One of them says he is sure that the vehicle was here the night before. You hope that they don't touch the housing to your thrusters. If they discover how hot it is, they'll know that you just stopped.

A warrior shouts and points out the dead Kubaz in the web. The intruders talk excitedly. Apparently they hadn't seen him in the darkness. They go to search his body, and begin squabbling over his credit disks.

One Kubaz takes your landspeeder and drives away. Others salvage the other landspeeders by cutting them down from the web. Then they, too, drive away.

Soon, only two Kubaz are left. They expertly climb up

the web and hack the legs off the ghost spydrs, bringing each leg back down and stacking them all on the back of the repulsor-lift sled. Clearly, only the legs of the ghost spydrs are used for food.

When the Kubaz have finished, the legs are tied down on the repulsor-lift and covered with a tarp, like logs.

You realize that you must strike soon. If you are to get a vehicle and go after your friends, you'll need to catch these Kubaz by surprise. You draw your weapon.

Just then, See-Threepio stands up, and raises his hands. "Yoo-hoo," he calls. "Are you looking for me?" Then he repeats the same words in Kubaz.

The Kubaz draw their weapons, and you realize what Threepio is doing: he's distracting them for you.

As they stalk toward Threepio, you draw your weapon and stand up.

You decide to try persuading the Kubaz (since it is wrong to shoot them in the back). You can persuade with Power, or without Power. If it doesn't work, you will have to fight.

To persuade the Kubaz workers (without Power): You say, "I don't like bug eaters, but if you drop your weapons and turn around real slow, you'll live to eat another fli." Threepio translates for you. Your charm# +1 is your confront#. Roll the 6-dice.

If your confront# is equal to or more than your roll#, add the difference +9 to your MP total. You have a gift for intimidating Kubaz workers. You may now proceed.

If your confront# is lower than your roll#, subtract the difference from your MP total. The Kubaz turn to you and raise their weapons. You must disarm them, both at once or one at a time (below).

To persuade the Kubaz (using Power)*: You must use your Persuasion Power. Your charm# + your Jedi# + your Power's mid-resist# is your confront#. Roll the 6-dice.

If your confront# is equal to or more than your roll#, add the difference +7 to your MP. The workers feel grateful that you let them live.

If your confront# is lower than your roll#, subtract the difference from your MP total. The Kubaz turn to you and raise their weapons. You must disarm them both at once or one at a time (below).

*Note: This counts as one of three Power uses you are allowed on this Mission.

To disarm the Kubaz (both at once): Choose your weapon. You aim for a branch right over the Kubaz. Your weapon# + your weapon's mid-range# is your confront#. Roll the 6-dice to shoot the branch.

If your confront# is equal to or more than your roll#, add the difference to your MP total. The branch falls and knocks down the Kubaz. You quickly confiscate their weapons. They are no longer a threat. You may proceed.

If your confront# is lower than your roll#, subtract the difference from your MP total. You miss the branch, and must now attempt to disarm the Kubaz one at a time (below).

To disarm the Kubaz (one at a time): Choose your weapon. Your weaponry# + your weapon's mid-range# is your confront#. Roll the 6-dice to fight.

If your confront # is equal to or more than your roll#, add the difference to your MP total. You've knocked the weapon out of one of the Kubaz's hands. After witnessing your awesome firepower, both Kubaz surrender immediately. You may proceed.

If your confront# is lower than your roll#, subtract the difference from your MP total. You must try again. Use the same confront# and repeat this confront until you have disarmed the Kubaz.

With the bug eaters out of the way, you take their hooded robes and pull them on. The Kubaz fear the radiation from solar flares, so when they go out by day they wear heavy robes that have metallic threads woven into them to protect them from unanticipated radiation. These robes cover your body, so that you and Threepio both look like Kubaz on casual examination.

You start up the landspeeder and follow the trail left by the other Kubaz. The long stalks of fungus have been broken and knocked over.

The path takes you deep into the forest, into shadowy realms. Above you, the giant spydrwebs are woven thick between the trees. They hang there like the great billowing sails of ships. Pale spydrs cling to the webs.

The trail leads you along a twisted path that has been cleared among the spydrwebs. At first, it seems like a random path. But soon you notice that on each great tree that the path follows, a single black line has been painted, marking the trail ahead.

You reach the Kubaz city, deep in the heart of the forest. Its great towers rise high among the trees. Cobwebs are strung between them.

As you draw near, you see dozens of Kubaz walking around. Those in green body armor are soldiers, carrying blasters and blaster rifles. The ones in yellow robes seem to be in charge of transportation, for they direct traffic in the city. Others in orange robes, like yours, perform menial labor, like unloading spydr legs from the sleds. The Kubaz, it seems, have a very ordered society.

Dozens of landspeeders have brought in loads of spydr legs. A man in yellow robes waves to you with a light stick, calling out in Kubaz and guiding you toward a dome where the spydr meat can be frozen. You don't want to go there — someone might get a close look at your face.

You lean forward so that the Kubaz doesn't see your human features beneath your deep hood. "Say something," you tell See-Threepio. "Get us out of here."

"Oh, I'm afraid I don't understand this dialect very well," Threepio says. "Kubindi is a newly discovered world."

"You're supposed to be fluent in ten billion dialects! Say *anything*."

"Uh, Ibikki zum abbimikim? Xiba sum cubizik," Threepio calls to the fellow in yellow.

The Kubaz shouts excitedly and waves you toward another dome, so that you don't have to line up behind the other landspeeders. You drive toward it.

"It worked!" Threepio rejoices. "You know, I never thought I had any talent for deception!"

Gratefully, you steer away from the vehicles and drive toward the secluded dome. "What did you say to him?" you ask Threepio.

"I asked for the nearest restroom. I said that you needed it badly."

You give See-Threepio a severe look, and pull up to the secluded dome. The two of you climb out.

"We have to make our way to the detention level," you inform the droid. "The others should be there."

The dome is something of a barn or incubation chamber. Copper-colored droids are working by the dozens. Luckily, the lowly labor droids don't even recognize that you aren't Kubaz. In the cool shade inside the dome there are huge wire cages filled with orange spydr eggs. Lights shine on the eggs to keep them warm. In some chambers, tiny ghost spydrs have hatched by the thousands. They scurry about like little silver crabs. The worker droids are tending the spydrs, feeding them ground meat, and spraying them with a hose that emits a fine mist.

You find a hydrolift down to the city, but you also find some downward tunnels. Hoping that you are less likely to meet others in the tunnels, you and Threepio begin walking down. The tunnels wind down and branch oddly. They have been hollowed by some giant insect, and are wider than they are tall. The farther you go, the more you are reminded of an insect hive for termytes or antz — *not* of the passages of a city.

Several worker droids wander the passage. Twice, you pass lone Kubaz workers walking upward. You keep your hoods low over your faces and hope that the Kubaz don't notice you, but both of them stare at Threepio and the odd way that he walks.

You go down several levels and find signs written in Kubaz next to each side passage. You had never realized how large a Kubaz hive could be. There must be dozens of branches, and each branch could house thousands of workers or traders or mechanics. Since no humans live among the Kubaz, there is no way that you're going to find Grubba without attracting attention.

"Here is the detention level," Threepio says as you reach one door in the tunnel. A guard droid stands beside the door, with a stunner in its hand.

You can lie to the droid without Power, lie with Power, fight the droid with a weapon, or seek to turn off its power supply (in hand-to-hand combat). Choose now.

To lie (without Power): You tell the droid that you have come to interrogate the human prisoners. Your charm# +1 is your confront#. Roll the 6-dice.

> *If your confront# is equal to or more than your roll#,* add the difference +5 to your MP total. The droid opens the door for you.

If your confront# is lower than your roll#, subtract the difference from your MP total. The droid doesn't believe you. You must combat it (below).

To lie (using Power)*: Choose your Persuasion or Deception Power. You tell the droid that you are here to translate during the interrogation of the human prisoners. Your charm# + your Jedi# + your Power's low-resist# is your confront#. Roll the 6-dice.

If your confront# is equal to or more than your roll#, add the difference +5 to your MP total. The droid opens the door for you.

If your confront# is lower than your roll#, subtract the difference from your MP total. The droid doesn't believe you. You must combat it (below).

*Note: This counts as one of three Power uses you are allowed on this Mission.

To combat the droid (with a weapon): Add your weaponry# +1 to your weapon's close-range# for your confront#. Roll the 6-dice to combat the droid.

If your confront# is equal to or more than your roll#, add the difference to your MP total. This droid is ready for the scrap heap.

If your confront# is lower than your roll#, subtract the difference from your MP total. Repeat this confront until the droid is disabled.

To combat the droid (hand-to-hand): You must grapple with it to turn off the power supply behind its back. Add your strength# to your skill# for your confront#. Roll the 6-dice to grapple with the droid.

> *If your confront# is equal to or more than your roll#,* add the difference to your MP total. The droid is out for the night. You may proceed.

> *If your confront# is lower than your roll#,* subtract the difference from your MP total. Repeat this confront until you have switched off the guard droid.

Once you have defeated the droid, add 20 MP to your total (30 MP for Advanced Level players).

You stand there for a moment, preparing yourself mentally. You hope that your friends are still alive. Above the door is a trip-bar, which you realize is some kind of alarm. To enter quietly, you must disable the alarm.

Note: If you persuaded the droid to open the door, you do not need to worry about the alarm. Simply proceed.

To disable the alarm: Your skill# +1 is your confront#. Roll the 6-dice.

> *If your confront# is equal to or more than your roll#,* add the difference to your MP total. You disable the alarm. You may proceed.

If your confront# is lower than your roll#, subtract the dif-ference from your MP total. Repeat the confront using the same confront# until you succeed.

You rush down the tunnel to the detention center. You see surveillance cameras up on the walls, but there is no way that you can blast them without drawing more atten-tion to yourself.

You enter a large room, where banks of security moni-tors are flashing warnings. Three menacing guard droids have taken defensive positions behind various desks and countertops. One of them shouts, "Warning: You have tres-passed onto the property of the Zabin Hive. In the name of Queen Zabin, surrender, human!"

"Look," you answer, "I just came here to get my friends back! I'm not looking for trouble."

One particularly fierce-looking droid stands up. He holds a laser cannon in his arms, and has power cartridges strapped over his chest in a bandolier. "Maybe you're not looking for trouble, mister," the droid says. "But you've found him!" The droid powers up the laser cannon, so that it whines as its cooling engines begin to heat. Vapors fill the room. "Go ahead, human —" the droid squints at you and dares you to fire, "complete my day!"

Another burly droid draws an enormous blaster and aims in your direction, shouting, "*Hasta la blaster,* baby!"

As you look at the brave droids you realize something is wrong. These Kubaz think you're the bad guy.

Threepio tugs at your elbow. "Excuse me," the droid

says. "But rather than a shoot-out, which I think you are certain to lose, might I propose a more diplomatic course of action?"

You look at See-Threepio. He is a diplomatic droid, well-versed in the customs and protocols of various alien species. "What would you suggest?"

"The Kubaz government is based upon hive organization," Threepio says. "If they think you are a warrior, they will treat you as an invader. Perhaps if would be better to present yourself as a diplomat, a foreign emissary, and appeal to their hive-honor."

"Oh," you say.

You look up at the deadly droids. "I am a diplomatic emissary from the Rebel Alliance," you say. "Take me to your leader."

You must convince the droids to take you to their leader. You can persuade them with Power or without Power. Choose now.

To persuade the guard droids (without Power): You say, "Look, I'll drop my weapon." Then you throw down your weapon. Your charm# +2 is your confront#. Roll the 6-dice.

If your confront# is equal to or more than your roll#, add the difference +3 to your MP total. You have a gift for charming Kubaz guard droids. They escort you to their queen.

If your confront# is lower than your roll#, subtract the difference from your MP total. One of the droids comes and slaps you with the butt of his weapon. He then drags you to his queen.

To persuade the Kubaz (using Power)*: Use your Persuasion Power. Your charm# + your Jedi# + your Power's low-resist# is your confront#. Roll the 6-dice.

If your confront# is equal to or more than your roll#, add the difference +3 to your MP total. You are much beloved by Kubaz guard droids. They escort you to their queen.

If your confront# is lower than your roll#, subtract the difference from your MP total. One of the droids comes and slaps you with the butt of his weapon. He then drags you to his queen.

*Note: This counts as one of three Power uses you are allowed on this Mission.

You are taken down long tunnels to Queen Zabin. You have never seen a female Kubaz before.

She sits in regal splendor upon her throne in a great room. Pet ghost spydrs behind her are held captive with chains of gold. Diamond rings adorn her gray snout, and her face is painted with graceful blue tattoos. Dozens of other Kubaz courtiers groom her. These courtiers are Kubaz children, dressed in splendid robes of white, with clustered gems at their collars. Around the queen, incense burns in silver braziers, so that the sweet smoke fills the hall.

You go to her and bow. Threepio translates for you.

"Wondrous Queen Zabin," you say, "great is the honor of your hive. I come to you as an emissary of the human worlds, seeking justice."

"I have heard of the human worlds," Queen Zabin says, "and have been anxious to establish trading partnerships with your people. The Zabin hive has long provided the finest-tasting ghost spydrs in the galaxy. Yet I have no direct outlet to the human worlds."

You wonder if you can make some kind of trade. Certainly, even in the Rebel Alliance, there must be some species who would want to purchase ghost spydr meat.

"You are anxious to trade as we are," you answer courteously. "Whole worlds are hungry for your goods. But there is a matter between us that must first be resolved."

"What is that?"

"I am on a diplomatic mission," you say. "A child, a young Hutt, has been taken from its family against its will. This is against the laws of our worlds. The penalties are most severe. A member of your hive brought the child here. We must return the child to its family."

Cautiously, Queen Zabin says, "I, too, love my children. I would regret if one were taken from me. I would seek vengeance. Would your laws punish *my* child, for taking the Hutt?"

You nod, and say, "Yes."

"On Kubindi," Queen Zabin says, "the laws of one hive do not apply to the next. I would not want my child punished. However, we also see the necessity of trade."

"What is it you want of me?" you ask.

"Go to my kitchens, and prepare me a human dish, an excellent dish, using the meat of my ghost spydrs. My master chefs will observe you, so that they might prepare it for human guests in the future. If the dish is excellent, you shall have your reward."

You want to shout, "But I'm not a cook!" Yet you know that you must prepare the meal. Hers is an odd request, but perhaps it does not seem odd to her alien mind.

Three fat Kubaz chefs escort you and Threepio to the kitchen — an enormous chamber. Thousands of spices line the walls, and none of them are familiar to you. Herbs and vegetables and exotic fruits abound, and everywhere there is spydr meat — huge slabs of white meat from the legs, delicate fingers of darker meat from the claws. Spydrs' eggs also abound. Some have been pickled, others are freshly laid. Some spydrs' eyes have been ground into a paste.

You consider what to do. You can think of only one fancy dish that you might make, a quiche-like soufflé. But you've never tried it with spydr meat, or with these strange spices.

Desperately, you get some fresh spydrs' eggs, poke them with a knife, and begin beating them with a wire whip. The chefs grunt, and their trunks squiggle as they mutter to one another. You boil a bit of spydr meat, both dark and light, and then taste it. Not bad . . . but a bit bland.

With Threepio's help, you find some oil and begin to fry it. The chefs stare in astonishment. You begin searching for spices on the shelves, opening each container of dried leaves or powder. As you do, you look behind you. Sometimes the chefs give little squeals of worry when you pick up a spice. Other times, they stroke their trunks thoughtfully. Yet on other occasions, they grunt with approval, or even sigh in wonder as you pour a new spice onto the frying spydr meat.

When the spydr meat has been blackened with spices, you pull it off the grill and chop it finely.

Then you search for something like cheese.

The funguses that grow in the Silver Forest of Dreams are many and varied, and some are rather pungent. You decide to try a concoction with four varieties. You chop up the funguses.

You oil a pan and put the meat and fungus at the bottom, then pour the beaten eggs on top.

This is the most important meal you may ever make.

To create the perfect alien soufflé: Double your skill# for your confront#. Roll the 6-dice to exercise your full culinary ability (and then some).

If your confront# is equal to or more than your roll#, add the difference +5 to your MP total. You just might have pulled this off. Your soufflé is just about ready for the oven.

If your confront# is lower than your roll#, subtract the difference from your MP total. Well, at least you tried. Hopefully that will be enough. You may proceed.

As you finish, you garnish the whole concoction with globs of spydrs' eyes. *Voilà!*

The chefs begin wriggling their trunks excitedly, shouting in Kubaz. One of them claps in spontaneous appreciation, weeping in wonder.

They grab the uncooked soufflé, preparing to rush it to their queen.

"Wait!" you shout. "First, we must bake it!"

The Kubaz chefs frown and pull at their trunks, definitely worried.

You heat an oven, place the soufflé inside, and cross your fingers, hoping it will rise, that it will cook just perfectly. You don't know how well it will rise when made with spydrs' eggs.

You wait twenty minutes, thirty. You peer through the glass. The glorious soufflé is rising! In fact, you've never seen one puff up like this. Already, it has formed a delicate head, and is beginning to turn a golden brown. In just a moment, it should be ready for tasting.

Just then, there is a dull rumbling sound, and the whole cavern shakes. Oh great, you think, I had to have my soufflé in the oven when a spaceship took off!

The soufflé falls in ruin.

Dejected, you pull it from the oven. Yet the aroma of it is surprisingly tantalizing. And you realize that the Kubaz queen has no idea what the soufflé was *supposed* to look like.

One of the Kubaz chefs rushes forward and quickly dashes off with the hot pan to the queen's audience room.

The queen watches you warily. You know full well that half of any good dish comes with the presentation. You raise your head proudly, give her an encouraging smile, and cross your fingers behind your back.

To please the queen with your dish, you may charm her without Power, or seek to persuade her with Power.

To persuade the queen (using Power)*: You must use your Persuasion Power or your Hypnotism Power. Your charm# + your Jedi# + your Power's mid-resist# is your confront#. Roll the 6-dice.

> If your confront# is equal to or more than your roll#, add 10 MP to your MP total. The queen smiles and eats another bite. The Kubaz chefs raise a shout of triumph. When she finishes her second bite, the queen offers, "With such grand talents, I would be well pleased if you would stay at Zabin hive and cook for me always!" You graciously decline.

> If your confront# is lower than your roll#, subtract the difference from your MP total. The queen politely takes a bite, and chokes it down. "An interesting flavor," she says coldly. "Is this how humans would eat my spydr meat?"

*Note: This counts as one of three Power uses you are allowed on this Mission.

To charm the queen (without Power): Your charm# +1 is your confront#. Roll the 6-dice.

> If your confront# is equal to or more than your roll#, add 10 MP to your MP total. The queen smiles and eats another bite. The Kubaz chefs raise a shout of triumph. When she finishes her second bite, the queen offers,

"With such grand talents, I would be well pleased if you would stay at Zabin hive and cook for me always!" You graciously decline.

If your confront# is lower than your roll#, subtract the difference from your MP total. The queen eats one bite, and chokes it down. "An interesting flavor," she says coldly. "Is this how humans would eat it?"

Satisfied, the queen accepts your dish. "You have won your reward," she says. "I decree that you and your friends are free to leave this hive, and that you will go with our blessings, and with a cargo full of spydr legs, as a gift to the Rebel Alliance."

"But what about the baby Hutt?" you ask. "What about justice!"

"The young Hutt is gone," Queen Zabin says. "The child left while you were cooking your dish." You suddenly remember the rumble of engines that ruined your soufflé. "My subject, Udin, assured me that the child was taken with the full approval of Imperial forces. Your politics are beyond my understanding. I dare not interfere in Imperial concerns."

You stare hard at the queen, astonished that she would do this. But you realize she is serious. She does not want to punish her child, and does not want to stir the anger of the Empire. So, for the moment, you are defeated.

Queen Zabin leans forward and says discretely. "Do not worry. Grubba was brought here only as bait. The bounty hunters still want their human prize. The bounty hunters will leave clues for you to follow."

This ends your Mission. You have not freed Grubba, but you know that the Bounty Hunters will set another trap — and next time you plan to get the young Hutt. Award yourself 90 MP (120 for Advanced Level Players).

THE AFTER-
MISSION

Night was falling on Kubindi when Solo, Luke, Leia, and the droids reached the *Millennium Falcon*. Above the ship, giant fyrefliis were soaring into the air, dancing like spinning moons a thousand feet in the sky.

Some Kubaz workers finished loading the cold compartments full of ghost spydr meat into the hold of the *Falcon*, and Solo nodded approvingly. It wasn't the same as getting Grubba back, but he might be able to sell this stuff to a broker and make a tidy profit from this trip.

"I'm sorry it didn't work out," Leia said to Solo. "I'm sorry most of all for Grubba. I can't imagine what the poor little Hutt is going through. He's got to be terrified, and so lonely."

"Oh, I wouldn't worry about him too much," Han said. "Hutts have pretty thick hides, and he's got some nasty bounty hunters for company. He's probably loving it."

"Still, I wish we could get him back," Leia said.

Luke went into the *Falcon*, only to come out a moment later.

"Han, we've got problems. A coded message came in from Rebel headquarters while we were gone. They say the hammerheads need our help on Ithor."

"That's not far from here," Solo said. "But what's the problem?"

"I don't know for sure," Luke said, "but while we were gone, the bounty hunters must have breached the security on the *Falcon*. On the monitor next to the message, I found this." Luke handed Solo a piece of clothlike paper.

Scrawled on the paper in red ink were four words: "See you on Ithor."

Aboard Dengar's ship, the *Punishing One*, Grubba the Hutt threw down his cards and laughed uproariously. "I win again. I now get eighty-two percent of any bounty that Jabba pays for me!" He reached into a container of baby ghost spydrs and popped one into his mouth. It wriggled frantically as he swallowed. "Mmmmm . . . when I have my own trading vessel, I will make a fortune selling these to my kin."

Dengar shook his head. *By now, I should know better than to play cards with the little monster,* he thought.

Eron voiced his sentiments exactly. "Too bad Queen Zabin wouldn't let us keep Han Solo. If she had, Grubba, you'd be heading back to Jabba by now . . . and we'd all be rich."

"I apologize to everyone for the inconvenience," Udin the Kubaz said. "I felt sure that my queen would side with us on this. We do, after all, represent the will of the Empire. Still, I must respect her wish to avoid upsetting the Rebels. I fear that I do not have a mind for politics."

"Yeah," Dengar said, "you can't blame her for wanting to please everyone. But we won't make this same mistake again. The trap is set. Han Solo won't escape from us on Ithor."

"Are you sure about that?" Eron asked. "The Ithorians haven't exactly been happy about the Imperial takeover of their world. Solo won't have to look hard to find friends."

"I'm sure," Dengar said. "I'm on good terms with the commander of the Ithorian herdship, *Tafanda Bay*. General Olan Dewes is his name. He owes me a big favor."

"How big?" Udin asked.

"Back when I was still working for the Empire, two colonels once wanted the same post. One of them hired a man to kill his rival — Olan Dewes. The Empire frowns on this kind of thing. So I spoiled the plan."

"You saved Dewes' life?" Eron asked.

"Let's just say that when I got finished, there was only one man who wanted the post. General Olan Dewes owes me. I'll take Han Solo and his Rebel friends as partial payment. He *won't* escape me again."

NEXT MISSION: ITHORIAN INVASION